This book belongs to:
D1103595

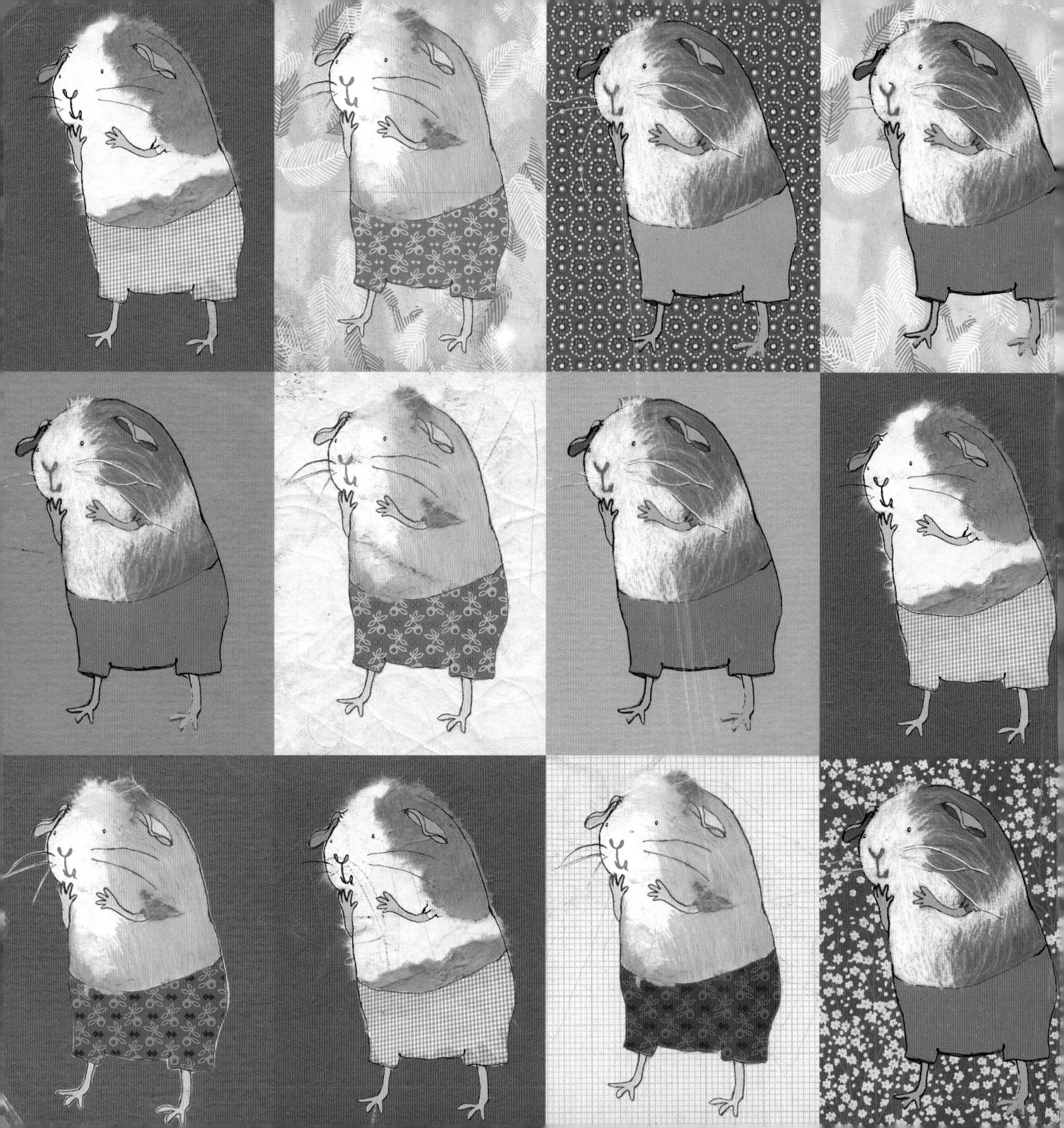

For Betty and Jack, with fond memories.

Nicola and Charlotte

OXFORD
UNIVERSITY PRESS

Great Clarendon Street, Oxford OX2 6DP

Oxford University Press is a department of the University of Oxford.
It furthers the University's objective of excellence in research, scholarship,
and education by publishing worldwide in

Oxford New York

Auckland Cape Town Dar es Salaam Hong Kong Karachi
Kuala Lumpur Madrid Melbourne Mexico City Nairobi
New Delhi Shanghai Taipei Toronto

With offices in

Argentina Austria Brazil Chile Czech Republic France Greece
Guatemala Hungary Italy Japan Poland Portugal Singapore
South Korea Switzerland Thailand Turkey Ukraine Vietnam

Oxford is a registered trade mark of Oxford University Press
in the UK and in certain other countries

Text and illustrations © Charlotte Middleton 2009

The moral rights of the author/illustrator have been asserted

Database right Oxford University Press (maker)

First published in 2009

This Bookstart edition first published in 2014

All rights reserved. No part of this publication may be reproduced,
stored in a retrieval system, or transmitted, in any form or by any means,
without the prior permission in writing of Oxford University Press,
or as expressly permitted by law, or under terms agreed with the appropriate
reprographics rights organization. Enquiries concerning reproduction
outside the scope of the above should be sent to the Rights Department,
Oxford University Press, at the address above

You must not circulate this book in any other binding or cover
and you must impose this same condition on any acquirer

British Library Cataloguing in Publication Data available

ISBN: 978-0-19-273997-1

2 4 6 8 10 9 7 5 3 1

Printed in China

Paper used in the production of this book is a natural,
recyclable product made from wood grown in sustainable forests.
The manufacturing process conforms to the environmental
regulations of the country of origin

CHARLOTTE MIDDLETON

presents

CHRISTOPHER Nibble

in a tale of dandelion derring-do!

OXFORD
UNIVERSITY PRESS

If there was one thing
Christopher Nibble loved
more than football,
it was . . .

eating dandelion leaves.
He ate
dandelion leaves...
at breakfast
time,
at lunch
time,
and at
dinner time.
And if Christopher felt
peckish between meals,
he ate...

more dandelion leaves!

But it was not just Christopher who liked dandelion leaves. Mr and Mrs Nibble liked them. His sister liked them. His friends liked them.

In fact. . . every guinea pig
in Dandeville loved dandelion leaves.
munch
munch
nibble
munch
nibble
All day long the happy
sound of munching and
nibbling filled the air. . .

until, that is,
dandelion leaves
began to
run out.

Dandelion dishes
were taken off
the menus, and
dandelion drinks
disappeared from
the shelves.

The last few leaves could be bought on the internet...

for a HUGE amount of money!

Soon the worst thing imaginable happened...
all o town the dandelions had been
munched thing more than bitten-down
stalks, and th ea pigs had to make do...

With chewy cabbage instead!

Just one dandelion was left but nobody knew about it, except Christopher Nibble. It happened to be growing right outside his bedroom window.

Christopher's mouth
watered at the sight of it.
But he knew he mustn't eat it,
or let anyone else eat it,
not if it was the last dandelion in town.

It might even be the last dandelion
in the whole world!
He thought hard and decided . . .

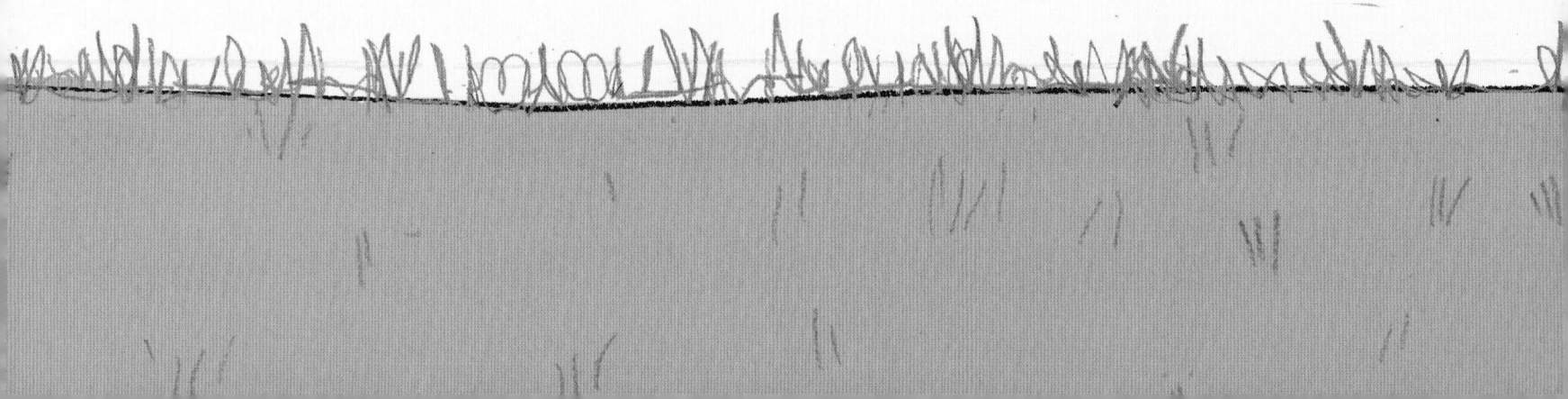

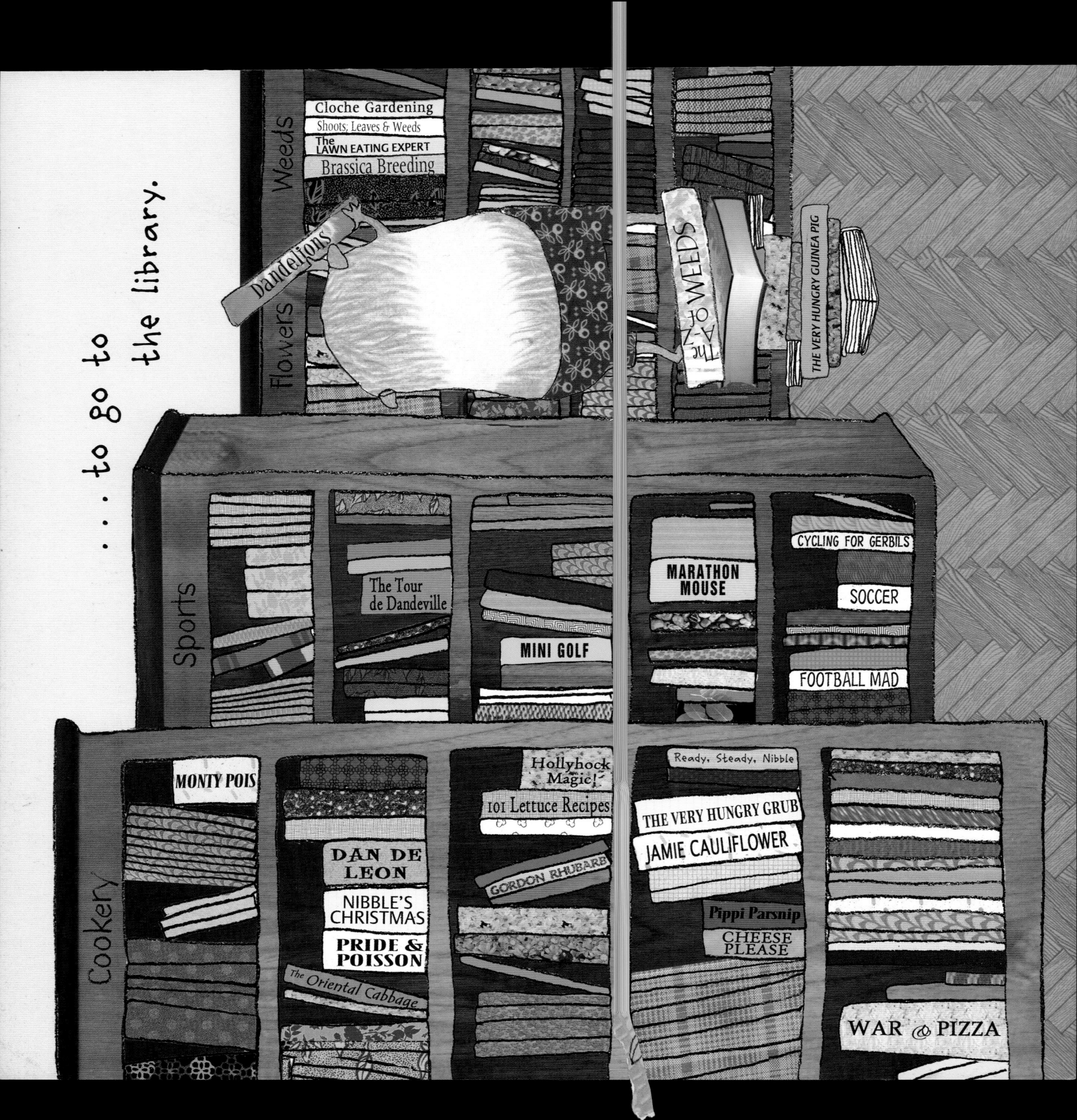
... to go to the library.
Flowers
Weeds
Cloche Gardening
Shoots, Leaves & Weeds
The LAWN EATING EXPERT
Brassica Breeding
Dandelions
The ART of WEEDS
THE VERY HUNGRY GUINEA PIG
Sports
The Tour de Dandeville
MINI GOLF
MARATHON MOUSE
CYCLING FOR GERBILS
SOCCER
FOOTBALL MAD
Cookery
MONTY POIS
DAN DE LEON
NIBBLE'S CHRISTMAS
PRIDE & POISSON
The Oriental Cabbage
Hollyhock Magic!
101 Lettuce Recipes
GORDON RHUBARB
Ready, Steady, Nibble
THE VERY HUNGRY GRUB
JAMIE CAULIFLOWER
Pippi Parsnip
CHEESE PLEASE
WAR & PIZZA

QUIET PLEASE!

He borrowed a book called 'Everything You Need to Know about Dandelions'

and he read it very carefully.

He found a little cloche to protect his dandelion. . .

and every day he watered it and picked off the bugs.

Every day he was very
good about not taking
even the tiniest
little nibble
while he . . .

waited,
and waited,
and waited.

Until, finally, his dandelion had grown the most beautiful white head of tiny seeds.

Very gently,
Christopher picked it
and carried it all
the way up
Daisy Chain Hill.
When he reached
the top...

he had just
enough puff to take
a deep breath and...

WOW!

The seeds filled the air...

and landed gently all over Dandeville.

At first nobody noticed.

But soon the new
plants started to sprout
fresh leaves.

And in no time at all Dandeville
was filled with the happy sound
of munching once more.

he still loves playing football.
munch
nibble
nibble

But now
there's
something
he loves just
as much
as eating
dandelions . . .
SEEDS

Christopher loves growing them!

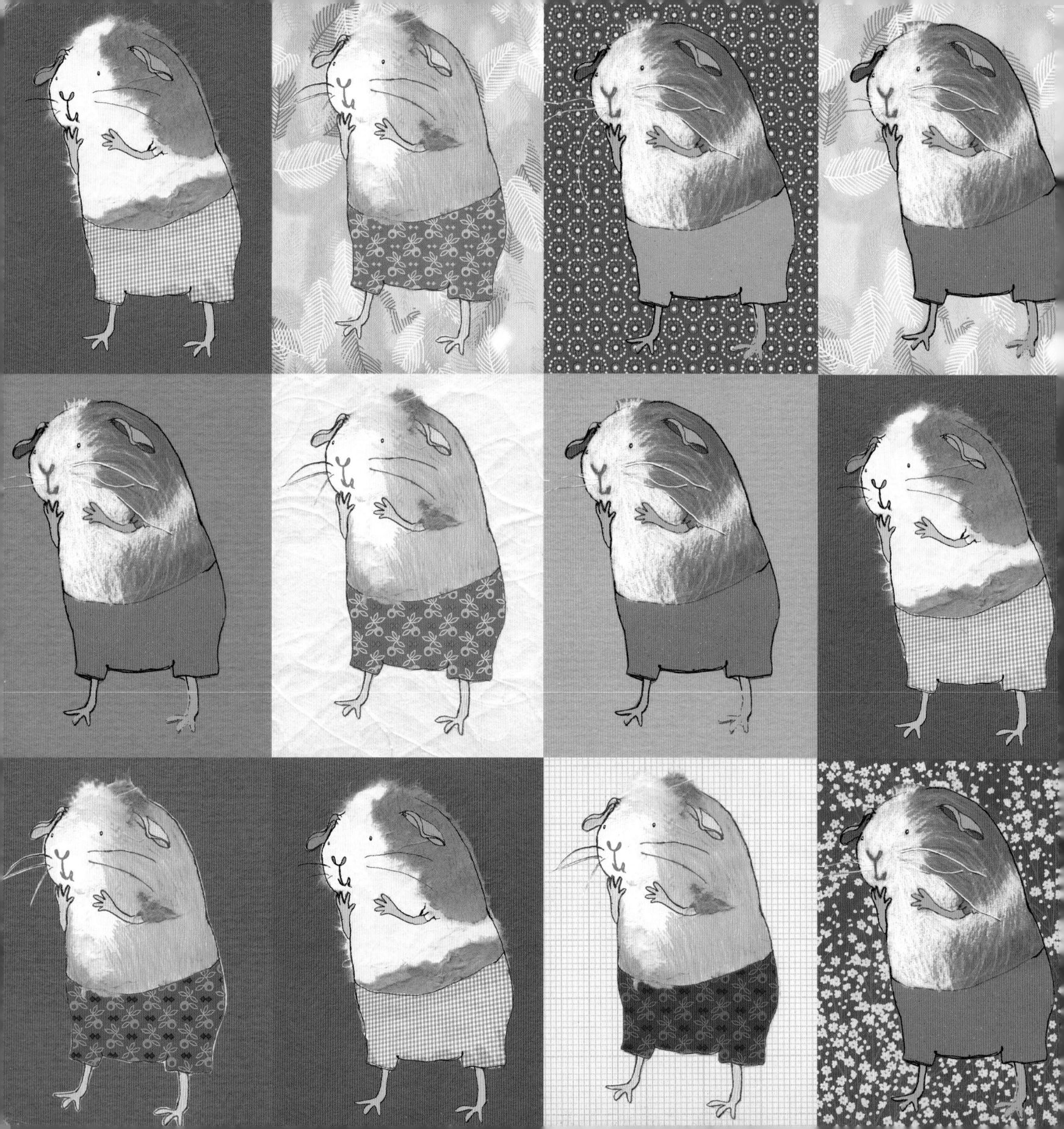

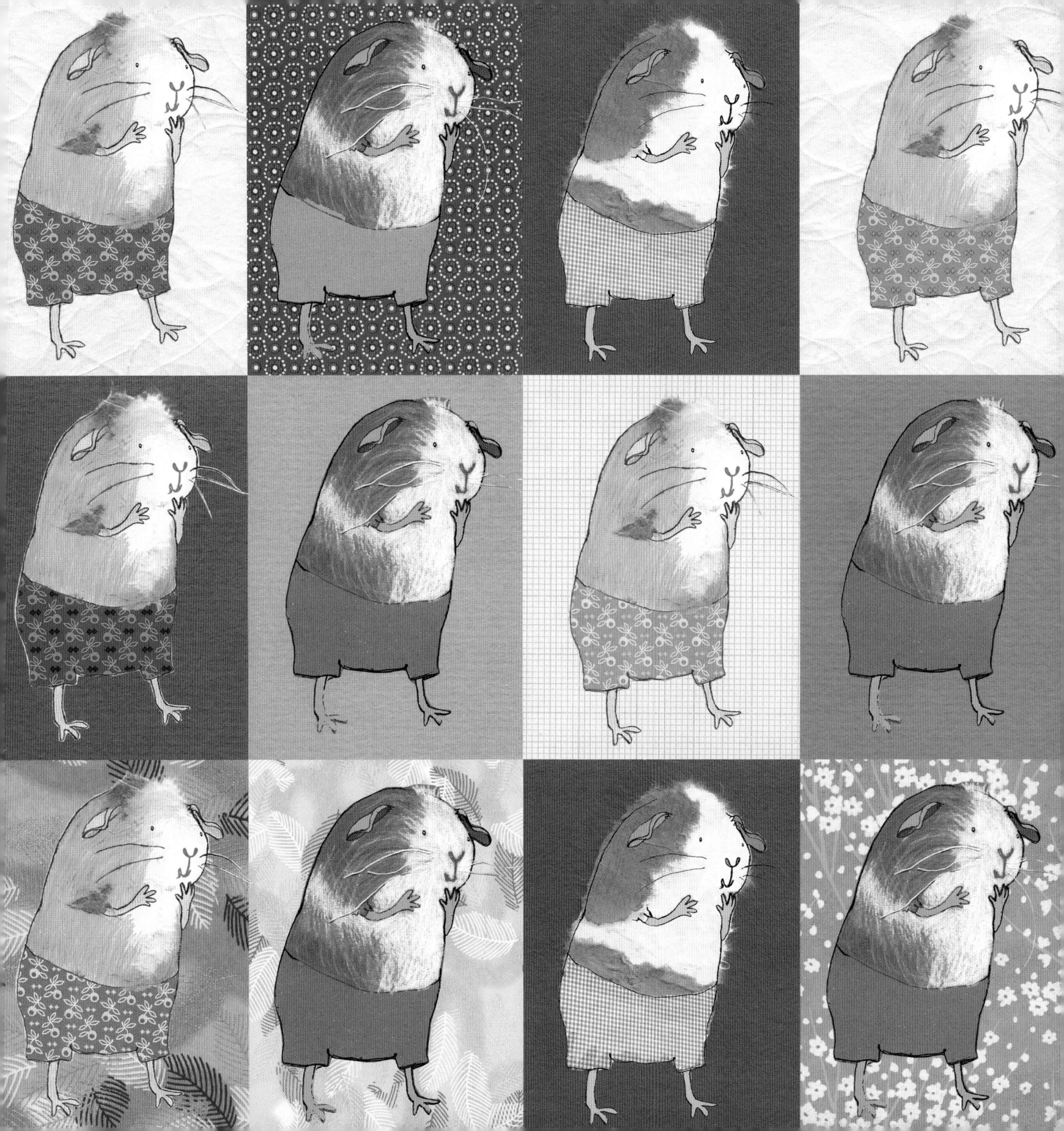

Picture books from Oxford are perfect for sharing...

978-0-19-273415-0 (pb)

978-0-19-279210-5 (pb)

978-0-19-275764-7 (pb)

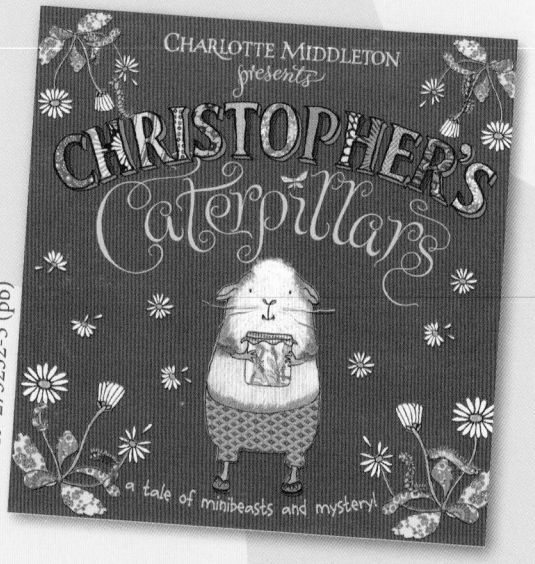

978-0-19-273232-3 (pb)

978-0-19-278018-8 (pb)

Available in all good bookshops or online at www.oxfordchildrens.co.uk